David Starr Jordan

The Call of the Twentieth Century; An Address to Young Men

in large print

MEGALI

David Starr Jordan

The Call of the Twentieth Century; An Address to Young Men

in large print

Reproduction of the original.

1st Edition 2024 | ISBN: 978-3-38732-877-6

Megali Verlag is an imprint of Outlook Verlagsgesellschaft mbH.

Verlag (Publisher): Outlook Verlag GmbH, Zeilweg 44, 60439 Frankfurt, Deutschland
Vertretungsberechtigt (Authorized to represent): E. Roepke, Zeilweg 44, 60439 Frankfurt, Deutschland
Druck (Print): Books on Demand GmbH, In de Tarpen 42, 22848 Norderstedt, Deutschland

THE CALL OF
THE TWENTIETH CENTURY

AN ADDRESS TO YOUNG MEN

BY DAVID STARR JORDAN

1903

To Vernon Lyman Kellogg

So
live that
your afterself—
the man you ought
to be—may in his time
be possible and actual. Far
away in the twenties, the thirties
of the Twentieth Century, he is awaiting
his turn. His body, his brain, his soul are in
your boyish hands. He cannot help himself. What will
you leave for him? Will it be a brain unspoiled by lust or
dissipation, a mind trained to think and act, a nervous
system
true as a dial in its response to the truth about you? Will
you,
boy of the Twentieth Century, let him come as a man among
men
in his time, or will you throw away his inheritance before
he has had the chance to touch it? Will you let him come,
taking your place, gaining through your experiences,
hallowed through your joys, building on them his
own, or will you fling his hope away,
decreeing, wanton-like, that the man
you might have been shall never
be?

The new century has come upon us with a rush of energy that no century has shown before. Let us stand aside for a moment that we may see what kind of a century it is to be, what is the work it has to do, and what manner of men it will demand to do it.

In most regards one century is like another. Just as men are men, so times are times. In the Twentieth Century there will be the same joys, the same sorrows, the same marrying and giving in marriage, the same round of work and play, of wisdom and duty, of folly and distress which other centuries have seen. Just as each individual man has the same organs, the same passions, the same functions as all others, so it is with all the centuries. But we know men not by their likenesses, which are many, but by differences in emphasis, by individual traits which are slight and subtle, but all-important in determining our likes and dislikes, our friendships, loves, and hates. So with the centuries; we remember those which are past not by the mass of common traits in history and development, but by the few events or thoughts unnoticed at the time, but which stand out like mountain peaks raised "above oblivion's sea," when the times are all gathered in and the century begins to blend with the "infinite azure of the past." Not wars and conquests mark a century. The hosts grow small in the vanishing perspective, "the captains and the kings depart," but the thoughts of men, their attitude toward their environment, their struggles toward duty,—these are the things which endure.

Compared with the centuries that are past, the Twentieth Century in its broad outlines will be like the rest. It will be selfish, generous, careless, devoted, fatuous, efficient. But three of its traits must stand out above all others, each raised to a higher degree than any other century has known. The Twentieth Century above all others will be *strenuous, complex*, and *democratic*. Strenuous the century must be, of course. This we can all see, and we have to thank the young man of the Twentieth Century who gave us the watchword of "the strenuous life," and who has raised the apt phrase to the dignity of a national purpose. Our century has a host of things to do, bold things, noble things, tedious things, difficult things, enduring things. It has only a hundred years to do them in, and two of these years are gone already. We must be up and bestir ourselves. If we are called to help in this work, there is no time for an idle minute. Idle men and idle women no doubt will cumber our way, for there are many who have never heard of the work to do, many who will never know that there has been a new century. These the century will pass by with the gentle tolerance she shows to clams and squirrels, but on those of us she calls to her service she will lay heavy burdens of duty. "The color of life is red." Already the fad of the drooping spirit, the end-of-the-century pose, has given way to the rush of the strenuous life, to the feeling that struggle brings its own reward. The men who are doing ask no favor at the end. Life is repaid by the joy of living it.

As the century is strenuous so will it be complex. The applications of science have made the great world small, while every part of it has grown insistent. As the earth has shrunk to come within our grasp, so has our own world expanded to receive it. "My mind to me a kingdom is," and to this kingdom all the other kingdoms of the earth now send their embassadors. The complexity of life is shown by the extension of the necessity of choice. Each of us has to render a decision, to say yes or no a hundred times when our grandfathers were called upon a single time. We must say yes or no to our neighbors' theories or plans or desires, and whoever has lived or lives or may yet live in any land or on any island of the sea has become our neighbor. Through modern civilization we are coming into our inheritance, and this heirloom includes the best that any man has done or thought since history and literature and art began. It includes, too, all the arts and inventions by which any men of any time have separated truth from error. Of one blood are all the people of the earth, and whatsoever is done to the least of these little ones in some degree comes to me. We suffer from the miasma of the Indian jungles; we starve with the savages of the harvestless islands; we grow weak with the abused peasants of the Russian steppes, who leave us the legacy of their grippe. The great volcano which buries far off cities at its foot casts its pitying dust over us. It is said that through the bonds of commerce, common trade, and common need, there is growing up the fund of a great "bank of human kindness," no genuine draft on which is ever left dishonored. Whoever is in need of help the world over, by that token has a claim on us.

In our material life we draw our resources from every land. Clothing, spices, fruits, toys, household furniture,—we lay contributions on the whole world for the most frugal meal, for the humblest dwelling. We need the best work of every nation and every nation asks our best of us. The day of home-brewed ale, of home-made bread, and home-spun clothing is already past with us. Better than we can do, our neighbors send us, and we must send our own best in return. With home-made garments also pass away inherited politics and hereditary religion, with all the support of caste and with all its barriers. We must work all this out for ourselves; we must make our own place in society; we must frame our own creeds; we must live our own religion; for no longer can one man's religion be taken unquestionably by any other. As the world has been unified, so is the individual unit exalted. With all this, the simplicity of life is passing away. Our front doors are wide open as the trains go by. The caravan traverses our front yard. We speak to millions, millions speak to us; and we must cultivate the social tact, the gentleness, the adroitness, the firmness necessary to carry out our own designs without thwarting those of others. Time no longer flows on evenly. We must count our moments, so much for ourselves, so much for the world we serve and which serves us in return. We must be swift and accurate in the part we play in a drama so mighty, so strenuous, and so complex.

More than any of the others, the Twentieth Century will be democratic. The greatest discovery of the Nineteenth Century was that of the reality of external things. That of the Twentieth Century will be this axiom in social geometry: "A straight line is the shortest distance between two points." If something needs doing, do it; the more plainly, directly, honestly, the better.

The earlier centuries cared little for the life of a man. Hence they failed to discriminate. In masses and mobs they needed kings and rulers but could not choose them. Hence the device of selecting as ruler the elder son of the last ruler, whatever his nature might be. A child, a lunatic, a monster, a sage,—it was all the same to these unheeding centuries. The people could not follow those they understood or who understood them. They must trust all to the blind chance of heredity. Tyrant or figurehead, the mob, which from its own indifference creates the pomp of royalty, threw up its caps for the king, and blindly died for him in his courage or in his folly with the same unquestioning loyalty. In like manner did the mob fashion lords and princes, each in its own image. Not the man who would do or think or help, but the eldest son of a former lord was chosen for its homage. The result of it all was that no use was made of the forces of nature, for those who might have learned to control them were hunted to their death. The men who could think and act for themselves were in no position to give their actions leverage.

When a people really means to do something, it must resort to democracy. It must value men as men, not as functions of a chain of conventionalities. "America," says Emerson, "means opportunity;" opportunity for work, opportunity for training, opportunity for influence. Democracy exalts the individual. It realizes that of all the treasures of the nation, the talent of its individual men is the most important. It realizes that its first duty is to waste none of this. It cannot afford to leave its Miltons mute and inglorious nor to let its village Hampdens waste their strength on petty obstacles while it has great tasks for them to accomplish. In a democracy, when work is to be done men rise to do it. No matter what the origin of our Washingtons and Lincolns, our Grants and our Shermans, our Clevelands or our Roosevelts, our Eliots, our Hadleys, or our Remsens, we know that they are being made ready for every crisis which may need their hand, for every work we would have them carry through. To give each man the training he deserves is to bring the right man face to face with his own opportunity. The straight line is the shortest distance between two points in life as in geometry. For the work of a nation we may not call on Lord This or Earl That, whose ancestors have lain on velvet for a thousand years; we want the man who can do the work, who can face the dragon, or carry the message to García. A man whose nerves are not relaxed by centuries of luxury will serve us best. Give him a fair chance to try; give us a fair chance to try him. This is the meaning of democracy; not fuss and feathers, pomp and gold lace, but accomplishment.

Democracy does not mean equality—just the reverse of this, it means individual responsibility, equality before the law, of course—equality of opportunity, but no other equality save that won by faithful service. That social system which bids men rise must also let them fall if they cannot maintain themselves. To choose the right man means the dismissal of the wrong. The weak, the incompetent, the untrained, the dissipated find no growing welcome in the century which is coming. It will have no place for unskilled laborers. A bucket of water and a basket of coal will do all that the unskilled laborer can do if we have skilled men to direct them. The unskilled laborer is no product of democracy. He exists in spite of democracy. The children of the republic are entitled to something better. A generous education, a well-directed education, should be the birthright of each one of them. Democracy may even intensify natural inequalities. The man who cannot say no to cheap and vulgar temptations falls all the lower in the degree to which he is a free agent. In competition with men alert, loyal, trained and creative, the dullard is condemned to a lifetime of hard labor, through no direct fault of his own. Keep the capable man down and you may level the incapable one up. But this the Twentieth Century will not do. This democracy will not do; this it is not now doing, and this it never will attempt. The social condition which would give all men equal reward, equal enjoyment, equal responsibility, may be a condition to dream of. It may be Utopia; it is not democracy. Sir Henry Maine describes the process of civilization as the "movement from status to contract." This is the movement from mass to man, from subservience to individualism, from tradition to democracy, from pomp and circumstance of non-essentials to the method of achievement.

Owen Wister in "The Virginian" says: "All America is divided into two classes,—the quality and the equality. The latter will always recognize the former when mistaken for it. Both will be with us until our women bear nothing but kings. It was through the Declaration of Independence that we Americans acknowledged the *eternal inequality* of man. For by it we abolished a cut-and-dried aristocracy. We had seen little men artificially held up in high places, and great men artificially held down in low places, and our own justice-loving hearts abhorred this violence to human nature. Therefore we decreed that every man should, thenceforth have equal liberty to find his own level. By this very decree we acknowledged and gave freedom to true aristocracy, saying, 'Let the best man win, whoever he is.' Let the best man win! That is America's word. That is true democracy. And true democracy and true aristocracy are one and the same thing. If anybody cannot see this, so much the worse for his eyesight."

Paucís vívat humanum genus: "for the few the race should live,"—this is the discarded motto of another age. The few live for the many. The clean and strong enrich the life of all with their wisdom, with their conquests. It is to bring about the larger equalities of opportunity, or purpose, that we exalt the talents of the few.

This has not always been clear, even the history of the Republic. My own great grandfather, John Elderkin Waldo, said at Tolland, Connecticut, more than a century ago: "Times are hard with us in New England. They will never be any better until each farm laborer in Connecticut is willing to work all day for a sheep's head and pluck," just as they used to do before the red schoolhouses on the hills began to preach their doctrines of sedition and equality. There could never be good times again, so he thought, till the many again lived for the few.

It is in the saving of the few who serve the many that the progress of civilization lies. In the march of the common man, and in the influence of the man uncommon who rises freely from the ranks, we have all of history that counts.

In a picture gallery at Brussels there is a painting by Wiertz, most cynical of artists, representing the man of the Future and the things of the Past. A naturalist holds in his right hand a magnifying glass, and in the other a handful of Napoleon and his marshals, guns, and battle-flags,—tiny objects swelling with meaningless glory. He examines these intensely, while a child at his side looks on in open-eyed wonder. She cannot understand what a grown man can find in these curious trifles that he should take the trouble to study them.

This painting is a parable designed to show Napoleon's real place in history. It was painted within a dozen miles of the field of Waterloo, and not many years after the noise of its cannon had died away. It shows the point of view of the man of the future. Save in the degradation of France, through the impoverishment of its life-blood, there is little in human civilization to recall the disastrous incident of Napoleon's existence.

Paucís vívat humanum genus: "the many live for the few." This shall be true no longer. The earth belongs to him who can use it and the only force which lasts is that which is used to make men free.

"Triumphant America," says George Horace Lorimer, "certainly does not mean each and every one of our seventy-eight millions. For instance, it does not include the admitted idiots and lunatics, the registered paupers and parasites, the caged criminals, the six million illiterates. In a sense, it includes the twenty-five to thirty million children, for they exert a tremendous influence upon the grown people. But in no sense does it include the whittlers on dry-goods boxes, the bar-room loafers, the fellows that listen all day long for the whistle to blow, those who are the first to be mentioned whenever there is talk of cutting down the force. It does not include those of our statesmen who spend their time in promoting corrupt jobs, or in hunting places for lazy heelers. It does not include the doctors who reach their high-water mark for professional knowledge on the day they graduate, or the lawyers who lie and cheat and procure injustice for the sake of fees.

"Most of these—even the idiots and criminals—do a little something towards progress. This world is so happily ordered that it is impossible for one man to do much harm or to avoid doing some good; and one of the greatest forces for good is the power of a bad example. Still it is not our bad examples that make us get on and earn us these smothers of flowery compliment.

"Some of us are tall and others short, some straight and others crooked, some strong, others feeble; some of us run, others walk, others snail it. But all, all have their feet upon the same level of the common earth. And America's worst enemy is he—or she—who by word or look encourages another to think otherwise. Head as high as you please; but feet always upon the common ground, never upon anybody's shoulders or neck, even though he be weak or willing."

So in this strenuous and complex age, this age of "fierce democracy," what have we to do, and with what manner of men shall we work? Young men of the Twentieth Century, will your times find place for you? There is plenty to do in every direction. That is plain enough. All the pages in this little book, or in a very large one, would be filled by a mere enumeration. In agriculture a whole great empire is yet to be won in the arid west, and the west that is not arid and the east that was never so must be turned into one vast market-garden. The Twentieth Century will treat a farm as a friend, and it will yield rich returns for such friendship. In the Twentieth Century vast regions will be fitted to civilization, not by imperialism, which blasts, but by permeation, which reclaims.

The table-lands of Mexico, the plains of Manchuria, the Pampas of Argentine, the moors of Northern Japan, all these regions in our own temperate zone offer a welcome to the Anglo-Saxon farmer. The great tropics are less hopeful, but they have never had a fair trial. The northern nations have tried to exploit them in haste, and then to get away, never to stay with them and work patiently to find out their best. Some day the possibilities of the Torrid Zone may come to us as a great discovery.

There is need of men in forestry; for we must win back the trees we have slain with such ruthless hand. The lumberman of the future will pick ripe trees and save the rest as carefully as the herdsman selects his stock. In engineering, in mining, in invention, there are endless possibilities. Every man who masters what is already known in any one branch of applied science, makes his own fortune. He who can add a little, save a little, do something better or something cheaper, makes the fortune of a hundred others. "There is always room for a man of force, and he makes room for many."

Andrew Carnegie once said that the foundation of his fortune lay in the employment of trained chemists, while other men made steel by rule of thumb. Trained chemists made better steel, just a little. They devised ways to make it cheaper, just a little, and they found means to utilize the slag.

All this means hundreds of millions of dollars, if done on a large enough scale.

There is no limit to the demands of engineering. A million waterfalls dash down the slopes of the Sierras. The patient sun has hauled the water up from the sea and spread it in snow over the mountains. The same sun will melt the snow, and as the water falls back to the sea it will yield again the force it cost to bring it to its heights. Thus sunshine and falling water can be transmuted into power. This power already lights the cities of California, and some day it may be changed into the heat which moves a thousand factories. All these are the problems of the Electrical Engineer. Equally rich are the opportunities in other forms of engineering. There is no need to be in haste, perhaps, but the Twentieth Century is eager in its quest for gold. The mother lode runs along the foothills from Bering Straits to Cape Horn. From end to end of the continent the Twentieth Century will bring this gold to light, and carry it all away. The Mining Engineer who knows the mountains best finds his fortune ready to his hand. Civil Engineers, Steam Engineers, Naval Engineers, whoever knows how to manage things or men, even Social Engineers, Labor Engineers, all find an eager welcome. There are never too many of those who know how; but the day of the rule of thumb has long since past. The Engineer of to-day must create, not imitate. And to him who can create, this last century we call the Twentieth is yet part of the first day of Creation.

In commerce the field is always open for young men. The world's trade is barely yet begun. We hear people whining over the spread of the commercial spirit, but what they mean is not the spirit of commerce. It is persistence of provincial selfishness, a spirit which has been with us since the fall of Adam, and which the centuries of whitening sails has as yet not eradicated. The spirit of fair commerce is a noble spirit. Through commerce the world is unified. Through commerce grows tolerance, and through tolerance, peace and solidarity. Commerce is world-wide barter, each nation giving what it can best produce for what is best among others. Freedom breeds commerce as commerce demands freedom. Only free men can buy and sell; for without selling no man nor nation has means to buy. When China is a nation, her people will be no longer a "yellow peril." It is poverty, slavery, misery, which makes men dangerous. In the words of "Joss Chinchingoss," the Kipling of Singapore, we have only to give the Chinaman

"The chance at home that he makes for himself elsewhere,
 And the star of the Jelly-fish nation mid others shall shine as fair."

Since the day, twenty-three years ago, on which I first passed through the Golden Gate of California, I have seen the steady increase of the shipping which enters that channel. There are ten vessels to-day passing in and out to one in 1880. Another twenty-five years will see a hundred times as many. We have discovered the Orient, and even more, the

Orient has discovered us. We may not rule it by force of arms; for that counts nothing in trade or civilization. Commerce follows the flag only when the flag flies on merchant ships. It has no interest in following the flag to see a fight. Commerce follows fair play and mutual service. Through the centuries of war men have only played at commerce. The Twentieth Century will take it seriously, and it will call for men to do its work. It will call more loudly than war has ever done, but it will ask its men not to die bravely, but to live wisely, and above all truthfully to watch their accounts.

The Twentieth Century will find room for pure science as well as for applied science and ingenious invention. Each Helmholtz of the future will give rise to a thousand Edisons. Exact knowledge must precede any form of applications. The reward of pure science will be, in the future as in the past, of its own kind, not fame nor money, but the joy of finding truth. To this joy no favor of fortune can add. The student of nature in all the ages has taken the vow of poverty. To him money, his own or others, means only the power to do more or better work.

The Twentieth Century will have its share in literature and art. Most of the books it will print will not be literature, for idle books are written for idle people, and many idle people are left over from less insistent times. The books sold by the hundred thousands to men and women not trained to make time count, will be forgotten before the century is half over. The books it saves will be books of its own kind, plain, straightforward, clear-cut, marked by that "fanaticism for veracity" which means everything else that is good in the intellectual and moral development of man. The literature of form is giving way already to the literature of power. We care less and less for the surprises and scintillations of clever fellows; we care more and more for the real thoughts of real men. We find that the deepest thoughts can be expressed in the simplest language. "A straight line is the shortest distance between two points" in literature as well as in mechanics. "In simplicity is strength," as Watt said of machinery, and it is true in art as well as in mechanics.

In medicine, the field of action is growing infinitely broader, now that its training is securely based on science, and the divining rod no longer stands first among its implements of precision. Not long ago, it is said, a young medical student in New York committed suicide, leaving behind this touching sentence: "I die because there is room for no more doctors." And this just now, when for the first time it is worth while to be a doctor. Room for no more doctors, no doubt, of the kind to which he belonged—men who know nothing and care nothing for science and its methods, who choose the medical school which will turn them loose most quickly and cheaply, who have no feeling for their patients, and whose prescriptions are given with no more conscience than goes into the fabrication of an electric belt or the compounding of a patent medicine. Room for no more doctors whose highest conception is to look wise, take his chances, and pocket the fee. Room for no more doctors just now, when the knowledge of human anatomy and physiology has shown the way to a thousand uses of preventive surgery. Room for no more doctors, when the knowledge of the microbes and their germs has given the hope of successful warfare against all contagious diseases; room for no more doctors, when antiseptics and anaesthetics have proved their value in a thousand pain-saving ways. Room for no more doctors now, when the doctor must be an honest man, with a sound knowledge of the human body and a mastery of the methods of the sciences on which this knowledge depends. Room for no more doctors of the incompetent class, because the wiser times demand a better service.

What is true in medicine applies also to the profession of law. The pettifogger must give place to the jurist. The law is not a device for getting around the statutes. It is the science and art of equity. The lawyers of the future will not be mere pleaders before juries. They will save their clients from need of judge or jury. In every civilized nation the lawyers must be the law-givers. The sword has given place to the green bag. The demands of the Twentieth Century will be that the statutes coincide with equity. This condition educated lawyers can bring about. To know equity is to be its defender.

In politics the demand for serious service must grow. As we have to do with wise and clean men, statesmen, instead of vote-manipulators, we shall feel more and more the need for them. We shall demand not only men who can lead in action, but men who can prevent unwise action. Often the policy which seems most attractive to the majority is full of danger for the future. We need men who can face popular opinion, and, if need be, to face it down. The best citizen is one not afraid to cast his vote away by voting with the minority.

As we look at it in the rough, the political outlook of democracy often seems discouraging. A great, rich, busy nation cannot stop to see who grabs its pennies. We are plundered by the rich, we are robbed by the poor, and trusts and unions play the tyrant over both. But all these evils are temporary. The men that have solved greater problems in the past will not be balked by these. Whatever is won for the cause of equity and decency is never lost again. "Eternal vigilance is the price of liberty," and in this Twentieth Century there are always plenty who are awake. One by one political reforms take their place on our statute books, and each one comes to stay.

In all this, the journalist of the future may find an honorable place. He will learn to temper enterprise with justice, audacity with fidelity, omniscience with truthfulness. When he does this he will become a natural leader of men because he will be their real servant. To mould public opinion, to furnish a truthful picture of the times from day to day, either of these ideals in journalism gives ample room for the play of the highest manly energy.

The need of the teacher will not grow less as the century goes on. The history of the future is written in the schools of to-day, and the reform which gives us better schools is the greatest of reforms. It is said that the teacher's noblest work is to lead the child to his inheritance. This is the inheritance he would win; the truth that men have tested in the past, and the means by which they were led to know that it was truth. "Free should the scholar be—free and brave," and to such as these the Twentieth Century will bring the reward of the scholar.

The Twentieth Century will need its preachers and leaders in religion. Some say, idly, that religion is losing her hold in these strenuous days. But she is not. She is simply changing her grip. The religion of this century will be more practical, more real. It will deal with the days of the week as well as with the Sabbath. It will be as patent in the marts of trade as in the walls of a cathedral, for a man's religion is his working hypothesis of life, not of life in some future world, but of life right here to-day, the only day we have in which to build a life. It will not look backward exclusively to "a dead fact stranded on the shore of the oblivious years," nor will its rewards be found alone in the life to come. The world of to-day will not be a "vale of tears" through which sinful men are to walk unhappily toward final reward. It will be a world of light and color and joy, a world in which each of us may have a noble though a humble part,—the work of the "holy life of action." It will find religion in love and wisdom and virtue, not in bloodless asceticism, philosophical disputation, the maintenance of withered creeds, the cultivation of fruitless emotion, or the recrudescence of forms from which the life has gone out. It is possible, Thoreau tells us, for us to "walk in hallowed cathedrals," and this in our every-day lives of profession or trade. It is the loyalty to duty, the love of God through the love of men, which may transform the workshop to a cathedral, and the life of to-day may be divine none the less because it is strenuous and complex. It may be all the more so because it is democratic, even the Sabbath and its duties being no longer exalted above the other holy days.

What sort of men does the century need for all this work it has to do? We may be sure that it will choose its own, and those who cannot serve it will be cast aside unpityingly. Those it can use it will pay generously, each after its kind, some with money, some with fame, some with the sense of power, some with the joy of service. Some will work hard in spite of vast wealth, some only after taking the vow of poverty.

Those not needed you can find any day. They lean against lamp-posts in platoons, they crowd the saloons, they stand about railway stations all day long to see trains go by. They dally on the lounges of fashionable clubs. They may be had tied in bundles by the employers of menial labor. Their women work at the wash-tubs, and crowd the sweat shops of great cities; or, idle rich, they may dawdle in the various ways in which men and women dispose of time, yielding nothing in return for it. You, whom the century wants, belong to none of these classes. Yours must be the spirit of the times, strenuous, complex, democratic.

A young man is a mighty reservoir of unused power. "Give me health and a day and I will put the pomp of emperors to shame." If I save my strength and make the most of it, there is scarcely a limit to what I may do. The right kind of men using their strength rightly, far outrun their own ambitions, not as to wealth and fame and position, but as to actual accomplishment. "I never dreamed that I should do so much," is the frequent saying of a successful man; for all men are ready to help him who throws his whole soul into the service.

Men of training the century must demand. It is impossible to drop into greatness. "There is always room at the top." so the Chicago merchant said to his son, "but the elevator is not running." You must walk up the stairs on your own feet. It is as easy to do great things as small, if you only know how. The only way to learn to do great things is to do small things well, patiently, loyally. If your ambitions run high, it will take a long time in preparation. There is no hurry. No wise man begrudges any of the time spent in the preparation for life, so long as it is actually making ready.

"Profligacy," says Emerson, "consists not in spending, but in spending off the line of your career. The crime which bankrupts men and nations is that of turning aside from one's main purpose to serve a job here and there."

The value of the college training of to-day cannot be too strongly emphasized. You cannot save time nor money by omitting it, whatever the profession on which you enter. The college is becoming a part of life. For a long time the American college was swayed by the traditions of the English aristocracy. Its purpose was to certify to a man's personal culture. The young man was sent to college that he might be a member of a gentler caste. His degree was his badge that in his youth he had done the proper thing for a gentleman to do. It attested not that he was wise or good or competent to serve, but that he was bred a gentleman among gentlemen.

So long as the title of academic bachelor had this significance, the man of action passed it by. It had no meaning to him, and the fine edge of accuracy in thought and perception, which only the college can give, was wanting in his work. The college education did not seem to disclose the secret of power, and the man of affairs would have none of it.

A higher ideal came from Germany,—that of erudition. The German scholar knows some one thing thoroughly. He may be rude or uncultured, he may not know how to use his knowledge, but whatever this knowledge is, it is sound and genuine. Thoroughness of knowledge gives the scholar self-respect; it makes possible a broad horizon and clear perspective. From these sources, English and German, the American University is developing its own essential idea,— that of personal effectiveness. The American University of to-day seeks neither culture nor erudition as its final end. It values both as means to greater ends. It looks forward to work in life. Its triumphs in these regards the century will see clearly. It will value culture and treasure erudition, but it will use both as helps toward doing things. It will find its inspiration in the needs of the world as it is, and it is through such effort that the world that is to be shall be made a reality. A great work demands full preparation. It takes larger provision for a cruise to the Cape of Good Hope than for a trip to the Isle of Dogs. For this reason the century will ask its men to take a college education.

It will ask much more than that,—a college education where the work is done in earnest, students and teachers realizing its serious value, and besides all this, it will demand the best special training which its best universities can give. For the Twentieth Century will not be satisfied with the universities of the fifteenth or seventeenth centuries. It will create its own, and the young man who does the century's work will be a product of its university system. Of this we may be sure, the training for strenuous life is not in academic idleness. The development of living ideals is not in an atmosphere of cynicism. The blasé, lukewarm, fin-de-siècle young man of the clubs will not represent university culture, nor, on the other hand, will culture be dominated by a cheap utilitarianism.

"You will hear every day around you," said Emerson to the divinity students of Harvard, "the maxims of a low prudence. You will hear that your first duty is to get land and money, place and fame. 'What is this truth you seek? What is this beauty?' men will ask in derision. If, nevertheless, God have called any of you to explain truth and beauty, be bold, be firm, be true. When you shall say, 'As others do, so will I; I renounce, I am sorry for it—my early visions; I must eat the good of the land, and let learning and romantic speculations go until some more favorable season,' then dies the man in you; then once more perish the buds of art and poetry and science, as they have died already in a hundred thousand men. The hour of that choice is the crisis in your history."

The age will demand steady headed men, men whose feet stand on the ground, men who can see things as they really are, and act accordingly. "The resolute facing of the world as it is, with all the garments of make-believe thrown off,"— this, according to Huxley, is the sole cure for the evils which beset men and nations. The only philosophy of life is that derived from its science. We know right from wrong because the destruction is plain in human experience. Right action brings abundance of life. Wrong action brings narrowness, decay, and degeneration. A man must have principles of life above all questions of the mere opportunities of to-day, but these principles are themselves derived from experience. They belong to the higher opportunism, the consideration of what is best in the long run. The man who is controlled by an arbitrary system without reference to conditions, is ineffective. He becomes a crank, a fanatic, a man whose aims are out of all proportion to results. This is because he is dealing with an imaginary world, not with the world as it is. We may admire the valiant knight who displays a noble chivalry in fighting wind-mills, but we do not call on a wind-mill warrior when we have some plain, real work to accomplish. All progress, large or small, is the resultant of many forces. We cannot single out any one of these as of dominant value, and ignore or despise the others. In moving through the solar system, the earth is falling toward the sun as well as flying away from it. In human society, egoism is coexistent with altruism, competition with co-operation, mutual struggle with mutual aid. Each is as old as the other and each as important; for the one could not exist without the other. Not in air-built Utopias, but in flesh and blood, wood and stone and iron, will the movement of humanity find its realization.

Don't count on gambling as a means of success. Gambling rests on the desire to get something for nothing. So does burglary and larceny. "The love of money is the root of all evil." This was said long ago, and it is not exactly what the wise man meant. He was speaking of unearned money. Money is power, and to save up power is thrift. On thrift civilization is builded. The root of all evil is the desire to get money without earning it. To get something for nothing demoralizes all effort. The man who gets a windfall spends his days watching the wind. The man who wins in a lottery buys more lottery tickets. Whoever receives bad money, soon throws good money after bad. He will throw that of others when his own is gone. No firm or corporation is rich enough to afford to keep gamblers as clerks.

The age will demand men of good taste who care for the best they know. Vulgarity is satisfaction with mean things. That is vulgar which is poor of its kind. There is a kind of music called rag-time,—vulgar music, with catchy tunes—catchy to those who do not know nor care for things better. There are men satisfied with rag-time music, with rag-time theatres, with rag-time politics, rag-time knowledge, rag-time religion. "It was my duty to have loved the highest." The highest of one man may be low for another, but no one can afford to look downward for his enjoyments. The corrosion of vulgarity spreads everywhere. Its poison enters every home. The billboards of our cities bear evidence to it; our newspapers reek with it, our story books are filled with it; we cannot keep it out of our churches or our colleges. The man who succeeds must shun, vulgarity. To be satisfied with poor things in one line will tarnish his ideals in the direction of his best efforts. One great source of failure in life is satisfaction with mean things. It is easier to be almost right than to be right. It is less trying to wish than to do. There are many things that glitter as well as gold and which can be had more cheaply. Illusion is always in the market and can be had on easy terms. Realities do not lie on the bargain counters. Happiness is based on reality. It must be earned before we can come into its possession. Happiness is not a state. It is the accompaniment of action. It comes from the exercise of natural functions, from doing, thinking, planning, fighting, overcoming, loving. It is positive and strengthening. It is the signal "all is well," passed from one nerve cell to another. It does not burn out as it glows. It makes room for more happiness. Loving, too, is a positive word. It is related to happiness as an impulse to action. The love that does not work itself out in helping acts as mere torture of the mind. The primal impulse of vice and sin is a short cut to happiness. It promises pleasure without earning it. And this pleasure is always an illusion. Its final legacy is weakness and pain. Pain is not a punishment, but a warning of harm done to the body. The unearned pleasures provoke this warning. They leave a "dark brown taste in the mouth." Their recollection is "different in the morning." Such pleasures, Robert Burns who had tried many of them says, are "like poppies spread," or "like the snow-falls on the river." But it is not true that they pass and leave no trace. Their touch is blasting. But true happiness leaves no reaction. To do strengthens a man for more doing; to love makes room for more loving.

The second power of vulgarity is obscenity, and this vice is like the pestilence. All inane vulgarity tends to become obscene. From obscenity rather than drink comes the helplessness of the ordinary tramp.

Another form of vulgarity is profanity. The habit of swearing is not a mark of manliness. It is the sign of a dull, coarse, unrefined nature, a lack of verbal initiative. Sometimes, perhaps, profanity seems picturesque and effective. I have known it so in Arizona once or twice, in old Mexico and perhaps in Wyoming, but never in the home, or the street, or the ordinary affairs of life. It is not that blasphemy is offensive to God. He is used to it, perhaps, for he has met it under many conditions. But it is offensive to man, insulting to the atmosphere, and destructive of him who uses it. Profanity and bluster are not signs of courage. The bravest men are quiet of speech and modest in demeanor.

The man who is successful will not be a dreamer. He will have but one dream and that will work itself out as a purpose. Dreaming wanes into sentimentalism, and sentimentalism is fatal to action. The man of purpose says no to all lesser calls, all minor opportunities. He does not abandon his college education because a hundred dollar position is offered him outside. He does not turn from one profession because there is money in another. He has his claim staked out, and with time he will only fill in the detail of its boundaries.

"Now that you are through college, what are you going to do?" asked a friend of a wise young man.

"I shall study medicine," was the grave reply.

"But isn't that profession already overcrowded?" asked the friend.

"Possibly it is," said the youth, "but I purpose to study medicine all the same. Those who are already in the profession must take their chances."

In this joke of the newspapers there is a sound philosophy. Men of purpose never overcrowd. The crowd is around the foot of the staircase waiting for the elevator.

The old traveller, Rafinesque, tells us that when he was a boy he read the voyages of Captain Cook, Le Vaillant, Pallas, and Bougainville, and "my soul was fired to be a great traveller like them, and so I became such," he adds shortly.

If you say to yourself: "I will be a traveller, a statesman, an engineer;" if you never unsay it; if you bend all your powers in that direction; if you take advantage of all helps that come in your way and reject all that do not, you will sometime reach your goal. For the world turns aside to let any man pass who knows whither he is going.

"Why should we call ourselves men," said Mirabeau, "unless it be to succeed in everything, everywhere. Say of nothing: 'This is beneath me,' nor feel that anything is beyond your power, for nothing is impossible to the man who can will."

Do not say that I am expecting too much of the effects of a firm resolution, that I give advice which would lead to failure. For the man who will fail will never take a resolution. Those among you whom fate has cut out to be nobodies are the ones who will never try!

Even harmless pleasures hurt if they win you from your purpose. Lorimer's old merchant writes to his son at Harvard: "You will meet fools enough in the day without hunting up the main herd at night." This plain business man's advice is worth every young man's attention.

The Twentieth Century will ask for men of instant decision, men whose mental equipment is all in order, ready to be used on the instant. Yes and no, right and wrong, we must have them labelled and ready to pack to go anywhere, to do anything at any time, or to know why we refuse to do it, if it is something we will not do. Ethelred the Unready died helpless a thousand years ago. The unready are still with us, but the strenuous century will grant them but short shrift.

The man of the Twentieth Century will be a hopeful man. He will love the world and the world will love him. "There is no hope for you," Thoreau once said, "unless this bit of sod under your feet is the sweetest for you in the world—in any world." The effective man takes his reward as he goes along. Nowhere is the sky so blue, the grass so green, the opportunities so choice as now, here, to-day, the time, the place where his work must be done.

"To-day is your day and mine," I have said on another occasion; "the only day we have, the day in which we play our part; what our part may signify in the great whole we may not understand, but we are here to play it, and now is the time. This we know: it is a part of action, not of whining. It is a part of love, not cynicism. It is for us to express love in terms of human helpfulness."

Whatever feeling is worthy and real will express itself in action, and the glow that surrounds worthy action we call happiness.

He will be a loyal man, considering always the best interests of him he serves, ready to lay down his life, if need be, for duty, ready to abandon whatever conflicts with higher loyalty, with higher duty.

In the economic struggles of to-day, well-meaning men are making two huge mistakes, which in time will undo whatever of good their efforts may accomplish. One of these is the struggle against education, the effort to limit the number of skilled laborers, and this in a free country where each man's birthright is the development of his skill. The other is the effort to destroy the feeling of personal loyalty on the part of the laborer. Half the value of any man's service lies in his willingness, his devotion to the man or the work. This old-fashioned virtue of loyalty must not be cheapened. The man whose service is worth paying for, gives more than his labor. He believes that what he does is right, and when anything goes wrong he will turn in and make it right. In the long run the laborer can get no more than he deserves, and disloyal labor is paving the way for its own subjugation. Unwilling service is a form of slavery, and unwilling employment is a slavery of the employer.

More than all this, the man in the Twentieth Century needs must be a man of character. It was said of Abraham Lincoln that he was a man "too simply great to scheme for his proper self." The man who schemes for his own advancement soon forfeits the support of others. He may lay pipes and pull wires, seeming for a little to succeed. "God consents, but only for a time." Sooner or later, if he lives to meet his fate, he finds his end in utter failure. And this failure is final: for those who have suffered will not help him again. Even rats desert a sinking ship. To be successful a man need take no heed for his own particular future. He will find his place in the future of his work.

In the ordinary business of life the smart man has had his day. He gives place to the man who can bring about results. Whatever the present menace of trust and monopoly, the business of the future must be conducted on large lines. The profits of the future will be the legitimate reward of economy, organization, and boldness of conception. To this end absolute honesty is essential to success. The merchant selling poor goods at high prices, an article which looks as good as the real thing but is something else, must give place to a larger system, with specialized service on a basis of absolute truthfulness. Business of a large scale must finally demand publicity and equity. Sooner or later even monopolies must grant this, whether we insist on it by statute or not. It is necessary for their own protection; for large structures cannot long stand on insecure foundations. In the long run trade is honest; for dishonest trade cuts its own throat.

Above all, because including all, the century will ask for men of sober mind. The finest piece of mechanism in all the universe is the brain of man and the mind which is its manifestation. What mind is, or how it is related to brain cells, we cannot say, but this we know, that as the brain is, so is the mind; whatever injury comes to the one is shown in the other. In this complex structure, with its millions of connecting cells, we are able to form images of the external world, truthful so far as they go, to retain these images, to compare them, to infer relations of cause and effect, to induce thought from sensation, and to translate thought into action. In proportion to the exactness of these operations is the soundness, the effectiveness of the man. The man is the mind, and everything else is accessory. The sober man is the one who protects his brain from all that would do it harm. Vice is our name for self-inflicted injury, and the purpose of vice is to secure a temporary feeling of pleasure through injury to the brain. Real happiness does not come through vice. You will know that which is genuine because it makes room for more happiness. The pleasures of vice are mere illusions, tricks of the nervous system, and each time these tricks are played it is more and more difficult for the mind to tell the truth. Such deceptions come through drunkenness and narcotism. In greater or less degree all nerve-affecting drugs produce it; alcohol, nicotine, caffeine, opium, cocaine, and the rest, strong or weak. Habitual use of any of these is a physical vice. A physical vice becomes a moral vice, and all vice leaves its record on the nervous system. To cultivate vice is to render the actual machinery of our mind incapable of normal action.

It is the brain's business to perceive, to think, to will, to act. All these functions taken together we call the mind. The brain is hidden in darkness, sheltered within a box of bone. All that it knows comes to it from the nerves of sense. All that it can do in this world is to act on the muscles it controls through its nerves of motion. The final purpose of knowledge is action. Our senses tell us what lies about us, that we may move and act, and do this wisely and safely. The sense-organs are the brain's only teachers so far as we know, the muscles are its only servants. But there are many orders which may be issued to these servants. Out of the many sensations, memories, imaginations, how shall the brain choose?

The power of attention fixes the mind on those sensations or impressions of most worth, pushing the others into the background. Past impressions, memory-pictures, linger in the brain, and these, bidden or unbidden, crowd with the others. To know the relation of all these, to distinguish present impressions from memories, realities from dreams,—this is mental sanity. The sane brain performs its appointed task. The mind is clear, the will is strong, the attention persistent, and all is well in the world. But the machinery of the brain may fail. The mind grows confused. It mistakes memories for realities. It loses the power of attention. A fixed idea may take possession of it, or it may be filled by a thousand vagrant impressions, wandering memories, in as many seconds. In this case the response of the muscles becomes uncertain. The acts are governed not by the demands of external conditions but by internal whims. This is a condition of mania or mental irresponsibility. Some phase of mental unsoundness is produced by any of the drugs which affect the nerves, whether stimulants or narcotics. They may help to borrow from our future store of energy, but they borrow at compound interest and never repay the loan. They give an impression of joy, of rest, of activity, without giving the fact; one and all, their function is to force the nervous system to lie. Each indulgence in any of them makes it harder to tell the truth. One and all, their supposed pleasures are followed by reactions, subjective pains as unreal as the joys which they follow. Each of them, if used persistently, brings incapacity, insanity, and death. With each of them use creates appetite. To yield once it is easier to yield again. The harm of some of them is slight. Tea, coffee, beer, claret, in moderate quantities, do but moderate harm, but all of them are without other effect on the nerves save to work them injury. White lies at the best are falsehoods. These are the white lies of physiology. In regard to each of these, the young man must count the cost. Count all the cost and be prepared to pay. The song of Ulrich von Hütten, when he gave his life for religious freedom, is worth applying to all other costly things. He sang:—

"'Ich habe gewagt mit Sinnen
Und trage des noch kein Reu.'"

"With open eyes have I dared it,
and cherish no regret."

For all indulgence in wine and coffee and tobacco you will have a bill to pay. Perhaps not a heavy bill. The indulgence may be worth the while, but if so, find out for yourself beforehand whether others have found it so. If you dare, dare with open eyes and cherish no regrets. For regret is the most profitless thing to cherish. There is nothing more distressing than remorse without will. The only hope in the world is to stop, and by the time that the inebriate comes to realize where he is, it is too late to stop.

"There is joy in life," says Sullivan, the pugilist, "but it is known only to the man who has a few jolts of liquor under his belt." To know this kind of joy is to put one's self beyond the reach of all others.

The joy of the blue sky, the bright sunshine, the rushing torrent, the songs of birds, "sweet as children's prattle is," the breath of the meadows, the glow of effort, the beauty of poetry, the achievement of thought, the thousand and thousand real pleasures of life, are inaccessible to him "who has a few jolts of liquor under his belt," while the sorrows he feels, or thinks he feels, are as unreal as his joys, and as unworthy of a life worth living.

There was once, I am told, a man who came into his office smacking his lips, and said to his clerk, "The world looks very different to the man who has had a good glass of brandy and soda in the morning." "Yes," said the clerk, "and the man looks different to the world."

And this is natural and inevitable, for the pleasure, which exists only in the imagination, leads to action which has likewise nothing to do with the demands of life. The mind is confused, and may be delighted with the confusion, but the confused muscles tremble and halt. The tongue is loosened and utters unfinished sentences; the hand is loosened and the handwriting is shaky; the muscles of the eyes are unharnessed, and the two eyes move independently and see double; the legs are loosened, and the confusion of the brain shows itself in the confused walk. And if this confusion is long continued, the mental deterioration shows itself in external things,—the shabby hat and seedy clothing, and the gradual drop of the man from stratum to stratum of society, till he brings up some night in the ditch. As the world looks more and more different to him, so does he look more and more different to the world.

A prominent lawyer of Boston once told me that the great impulse to total abstinence came to him when a young man, from hearing his fellow lawyers talking over their cups. The most vital secrets of their clients' business were made public property when their tongues were loosened by wine; and this led him to the firm resolution that nothing should go into his mouth which would prevent him from keeping it closed unless he wanted to open it. The time will come when the only opening for the ambitious man of intemperate habits will be in politics. It is rapidly becoming so now.

Private employers dare not trust their business to the man who drinks. The great corporations dare not. He is not wanted on the railroads. The steamship lines have long since cast him off. The banks dare not use him. He cannot keep accounts. Only the people, long-suffering and generous, remain as his resource. For this reason municipal government is his specialty; and while this patience of the people lasts, our cities will breed scandals as naturally as our swamps breed malaria. Already the business of the century recognizes the truth of all this. The bonding companies ask, before they sign a contract, whether the official in question uses liquor, what kind of liquor, whether he smokes, gambles, or in other ways so conducts himself that in five years he will be less of a man than he is now.

The great corporations ask the same questions as to all their employees. Even these organizations called "soulless" know the value of men, and that the vices of to-day must be reckoned at compound interest and charged against their estimate of the young man's future. The Twentieth Century must be temperate; for only sober men can bear the strain of its enterprises.

Equally dangerous is the search for the joys of love by those who would shirk all love's responsibilities. Just as honest love is the most powerful influence that can enter into a man's life, so is love's counterfeit the most disintegrating. Happiness cannot spring from the ashes of lust. Love looks toward the future. Its glory is its altruism. To shirk responsibility is to destroy the home. The equal marriage demands equal purity of heart, equal chastity of intention. Open vice brings with certainty disease and degradation. Secret lust comes to the same end, but all the more surely because the folly of lying is added to other sources of decay. That society is so severe in its condemnation of "the double life" is an expression of the bitterness of its experience. The real character of a man is measured by the truth he shows to women. His ideal of womankind is gauged by the character of the woman he seeks.

In general, the sinner is not the man who sets out in life to be wicked. Few men are born wicked; many are born weak. False ideas of manliness; false conceptions of good fellowship, which false ideas of the relationship of men and women give, wreck many a young man of otherwise good intentions. The sinner is the man who cannot say no. The fall through vice to sin is a matter of slow transition. One virtue after another is yielded up as the strain on the will becomes too great. In Kipling's fable of Parenness, the demon appears before the clerk in the Indian service, who has been too long a good fellow among the boys. It asks him to surrender three things in succession: his trust in man, his faith in woman, then the hopes and ambitions of his childhood. When these are given up, as they must be in the life of dissipation, the demon leaves him in exchange a little crust of dry bread. Bare existence without joy or hope is all that the demon can give when the forces of life are burned out.

In our colleges, the one ethical principle kept before the athlete by his associates is this: Never break training rules. The pitcher who smokes a cigarette throws away his game. The punter who spends the night at a dance loses his one chance of making a goal. The sprinter who takes the glass of convivial beer breaks no record. His record breaks him. Some day we shall realize that the game of life is more than the game of foot-ball. We have work every day more intricate than pitching curves, more strenuous than punting the ball. We must keep in trim for it. We must hold ourselves in repair. We must remember training rules. When this is done, we shall win not only games and races, but the great prizes of life. Almost half the strength of the men of America is now wasted in dissipation, gross or petty, in drink or smoke. This strength would be saved could we remember training rules. Through the training rules of our fathers we have come to consider as part of our inheritance the Puritan Conscience. As the success of our nation is built upon this conscience, so in like fashion depends upon it the success of our daily life.

I had a friend once, a mining man of some education, who made his fortune in bonanza days in Nevada, and who drank up what he had made with the boys who have long since passed away. As a hopeless sot he visited the gold cure at Los Gatos. Not finding much relief, he walked over to Palo Alto to borrow of me his fare to San Francisco. He said that he was going to pawn his goods for a fare to Nevada, where he meant to kill himself. Whether he did so or not, I do not know; for ten years have gone by and I have never heard of him again.

As he sat in my room, haggard, bloodshot, ragged, gin-flavored, a little boy who had then never known sin, came in, and being no respecter of persons, took him for a man and offered him his hand.

Being taken for a man, brought him back his manhood for a moment. The visions of evil left him, and from Dickens' poem of "The Children" he repeated almost to himself these words:—

"'I know now how Jesus could liken The Kingdom of God to a child.'"

The old scene came back to him. When the Master was teaching, the children crowded about him, and there were those who would send them away. But the Master said, "No, let the little children come unto me, and do not forbid them; for of such is the Kingdom of Heaven." And again he said, "The Kingdom of Heaven is within you." And again those whose services the Lord of the centuries could use, he likened to little children.

And of the many ways in which this likeness can be used this is one. The child is born with brain and nervous system adequate to its many purposes in life, if it is suffered to grow naturally, to become what God meant it to be. There are not many children of sin not made so by vice, intemperance, lust, and obscenity. They are victims of their elders' folly, of our carelessness as to their environment. Half the troubles of men of our race come through self-inflicted injury to the nervous system. We are tormented by the "fool-killer." If we could revert to the child's simple purity, the free movement of its machinery of life, we should find ourselves in a new heaven on a new earth. We could understand for ourselves part of what the Master meant. We should know now how Jesus could liken the Kingdom of God to a child.

All forms of subjective enjoyment, all pleasures that begin and end with self, unrelated to external things, are insane and unwholesome, destructive alike to rational enjoyment and to effectiveness in life. And this is true of spurious emotions alike, whether the pious ecstasies of a half-starved monk, the neurotic imaginings of a sentimental woman, or the riots of a debauchee. He is the wise man who for all his life can keep mind and soul and body clean.

"I know of no more encouraging fact," says Thoreau, "than the ability of a man to elevate his life by conscious endeavor. It is something to paint a particular picture, or to carve a statue, and so make a few objects beautiful. It is far more glorious to carve and paint the very atmosphere and medium through which we look. This morally we can do."

If it were ever my fortune in speaking to young men to become eloquent, with the only real eloquence there is, the plain speaking of a living truth, this I would say:—

Your first duty in life is toward your after-self. So live that your after-self—the man you ought to be—may in his time be possible and actual. Far away in the twenties, the thirties, of the Twentieth Century he is awaiting his turn. His body, his brain, his soul are in your boyish hands. He cannot help himself. What will you leave for him? Will it be a brain unspoiled by lust or dissipation, a mind trained to think and act, a nervous system true as a dial in its response to the truth about you? Will you, boy of the Twentieth Century, let him come as a man among men in his time, or will you throw away his inheritance before he has had the chance to touch it? Will you turn over to him a brain distorted, a mind diseased, a will untrained to action, a spinal cord grown through and through with the devil grass of that vile harvest we call wild oats? Will you let him come, taking your place, gaining through your experiences, hallowed through your joys, building on them his own, or will you fling his hope away, decreeing wanton-like that the man you might have been shall never be?

This is your problem in life, the problem of more importance to you than any or all others. How will you solve it? Will you meet it as a man or as a fool? When you answer this, we shall know what use the Twentieth Century can make of you.

"Death is a thing cleaner than Vice," Owen Wister tells us, and in the long run it is more profitable.

Charles R. Brown tells us of the old physician showing the physical effects of vice in the Museum of Pathology. "Almighty God writes a very plain hand." This is what he said. In every failure as in every success in the Twentieth Century, this plain hand can be plainly traced. "By their long memories the gods are known." This is an older form of the very same great lesson, the "goodness and severity of God."

Those who control the spiritual thought of the Twentieth Century will be religious men. They will not be religious in the fashion of monks, ascetics, mystic dreamers, or emotional enthusiasts. They will not be active in debating societies, discussing the intricacies of creeds. Neither will they be sticklers as to details in religious millinery. They will be simple, earnest, God-fearing, because they have known the God that makes for righteousness. Their religion of the Twentieth Century will be its working theory of life. It will be expressed in simple terms or it may not be expressed at all, but it will be deep graven in the heart. In wise and helpful life it will find ample justification. It will deal with the world as it is in the service of "the God of things as they are." It will find this world not "a vale of tears," a sink of iniquity, but a working paradise in which the rewards of right doing are instant and constant. It will find indeed that "His service is perfect freedom," for all things large or small within the reach of human effort are done in His way and in His way only.

Whittier tells us of the story of the day in Connecticut in 1780, when the horror of great darkness came over the land,

and all men feared the dreaded Day of Judgment had come at last.

The Legislature of Connecticut, "dim as ghosts" in the old State House, wished to adjourn to put themselves in condition for the great assizes. Meanwhile, Abraham Davenport, representative from Stamford rose to say:—

"This may well be
The Day of Judgment for which the world awaits;
But be it so or not, I only know
My present duty and my Lord's command
To occupy till He come.
So at the Post where He hath set me in His Providence,
I choose for one to meet Him face to face.
Let God do His work. We will see to ours."

Then he took up a discussion of an act relating to the fisheries of alewife and shad, speaking to men who felt them obliged to stand by their duty, though never expecting to see shad, or alewife, or even Connecticut again.

"Glad did I live and gladly die,
And I lay me down with a will."

This was Stevenson's word. "Let God do His work; we will see to ours." And in whatever part of God's Kingdom we men of the Twentieth Century may find ourselves, we shall know that we are at home. For the same hand that made the world and the ages created also the men in whose hands the final outcome of the wayward centuries finds its place within the Kingdom of Heaven.